MY MOM IS HAVING SURGERY

A KIDNEY STORY

Be cool ;
Share your
spare oo
☺

Brenda E. Cortez

by Brenda E. Cortez

Cover and interior design by Cecille Kaye Gumadan
Illustrations by Dindo Contento
Editing by Marla McKenna

Published in the United States of America
My Mom is Having Surgery
ISBN: 978-0-9993601-0-1

DONATE LIFE

donatelife.net

Help someone in need, even if you don't know them. Register today to be a donor.

In memory of Donna Glover, whose family graciously made the decision to donate her organs in their time of sorrow. Donna's gift of life has helped save five lives.

I'm very proud my mom decided to be a living kidney donor! Even though it was a bit scary to see Mom in the hospital, she is feeling great and so is Lizzy's mom.

We talked about the kidney donation at school and I said to my class, "My Mom did a really great thing and helped another person that was in need. I am so proud of her!"

Lizzy and I decided to do our fifth grade science projects about the kidney transplant to help our class understand the process better. My project explained kidney donation, and Lizzy's explained the kidney transplant process for the recipient. We hope our information convinced others to be an organ donor!

My name is Kailey and my mom is going to have surgery. I am scared because I don't really know what happens during surgery. I wonder how long it will take and if it hurts? My brother and I don't want anything to happen to Mom because we love her and need her.

I told my mom how worried I am, but she gently explained, "People have surgery every day Kailey, and the doctors and nurses go to school for a very long time so they know what to do. They have special training and take many tests before they are allowed to work in the hospital." She also added, "After the surgery they will keep a very close watch on me."

I replied happily, "Oh good, this makes me feel better."

"It is their job to help look after me, and make sure I get well as quickly as possible." Mom added reassuringly.

My mom's surgery is a little different than others because she has chosen to have the surgery to help another mom she hardly knows. My mom is giving away one of her kidneys, but most people call it donating a kidney or a kidney donation. She is donating her kidney to Lizzy's mom, Pam. Lizzy and I go to school together and she is in my fifth grade class.

Lizzy told me, "My mom needs to get a new kidney or she could become very sick. She has a kidney disease, which means her kidneys aren't doing what they are supposed to do."

Our teacher, Mrs. Smith, was talking to our class about the surgery and explained, "Kidneys are very important in keeping us healthy, but we can live with only one kidney. Some people are born with only one, while others may lose one due to an injury or they will donate one to a person in need."

I asked Mrs. Smith, "What does a kidney do for us?"

She answered, "The kidneys help clean the blood in our bodies and make sure we have the right amount of fluids. They also help keep our bones strong."

People say my mom is doing a brave thing and giving a very great gift to Pam. I heard a lady say to my mom how amazed she was that Mom could donate a body part to someone she barely knew. Most people say they don't know if they could be like her and give a part of their body away to a person who is not family.

Our neighbor Sue was at our house visiting the other day and she asked my mom, "What if someone in your family needed a kidney someday, but you already gave one away?"

My mom kindly replied, "You can't live your life worrying about things you have no control over. I know in my heart I am meant to do this, and I want to help someone by doing what I hope someone would do for me or my family."

My mom has always taught us to treat people the way we want to be treated, and do things for others that we would want them to do for us.

Today is the day of Mom's surgery and I am nervous for her. Grandma Judy is taking me and my brother Kyle to the hospital to see her after surgery. I asked Grandma, "Is Mom going to be awake during the surgery?"

She stated, "No Kailey, your mom is being put to sleep by a special doctor called an anesthesiologist, so she won't feel anything. They will give her special medicine through an IV, which is a small tube attached to her arm. The medicine will make her sleep for as long as the surgery takes."

We don't get to see my mom right away after surgery, because Grandma told me she will go to the recovery room where nurses will watch her and make sure she wakes up feeling okay. They also make sure she isn't scared when she wakes up, because she will be very sleepy and may not realize where she is right away.

"Can we see her yet?" I questioned anxiously.

"After she is awake your mom will go to her own room in the hospital, and then we can finally see her!" exclaimed Grandma.

The hospital is a very big place, with many rooms for the patients who have to stay here. When we first got to the hospital, we met up with my dad and Lizzy's family in the waiting room. That's a place where family and visitors can sit and talk or watch TV while they wait for someone to come out of surgery.

The doctor just came in and said to my dad, "The surgery went well and your wife is in the recovery room so she can start waking up. Once she awakens the nurses will wheel her to her room. Then she can see you."

Dad explained to Kyle and me, "Mom gets to stay in her bed because the bed has wheels on it, and they can just wheel her around."

Kyle laughed and said, "That is pretty cool!"

We just got to my mom's room and I thought she would be awake, but she actually fell back asleep. A nurse named Richelle is in the room to help her, so I asked, "Why is my mom sleeping?"

She replied kindly, "When someone is put to sleep for surgery it makes them very tired, so even though they wake up they are still exhausted and will sleep a lot. Your mom needs extra sleep today because she is exhausted from everything her body just went through. Her body needs to heal and get better, which will require plenty of rest for the next few weeks."

"Mom is awake!" I exclaimed as I also wondered why she looked so pale. The nurse reassured me that is normal after surgery. "But why does she still have the IV in her arm?" I questioned.

"That's how she receives the medicine to help her with pain," replied the nurse as she explained the IV has a skinny tube that runs from my mom's arm to a bag with liquid in it. The bag hangs on a special tower with wheels so when she gets up later to walk or use the bathroom, the tower can go along with her.

"I've never seen medicine look like this before," I said to my mom.

"When can you come home?" Kyle quietly asked.

Mom replied, "I have to stay in the hospital for a few days because my surgery is considered a major operation. Some surgeries don't take as long as others, so those people may go home the same day or only stay in the hospital a day or two. Others who are very sick may have to stay for a long time."

My mom is feeling better every day but sometimes her tummy feels yucky and she feels like fainting. The doctors and nurses come and check on her a lot.

Mom said, "I wish the nurses wouldn't come and check on me so much, because they wake me up when I am sleeping to ask how I feel," as she showed us a special button she can press to call for help if she needs anything. The nurses also make her get out of bed and walk around a few times a day, even though she doesn't really feel like it.

Nurse Richelle told me that walking around helps people heal quicker. My mom has walked down to Pam's room a few times to see how she is doing with her new kidney.

I don't mind going to the hospital every day because I like to see my mom. I also like that Grandma takes me to the cafeteria where they sell good food and really yummy smoothies! The hospital brings meals to my mom's room for her to eat, but she hasn't eaten very much the last few days.

I curiously asked nurse Richelle, "Is it all right that my mom isn't eating much?"

She replied, "It is normal that your mom is not very hungry. Her body is adjusting to everything it went through during surgery." She also added, "Even though she gets medicine, she still has a lot of pain that causes her not to feel very hungry."

Surgery isn't easy and is actually scary for most people, but moms, dads, grandmas, grandpas, and kids all around the world have surgery every day.

"Yay, Mom is coming home today!" I exclaimed.

She has been in the hospital for four nights but is feeling well enough now to come home! Dad suggested we make a welcome home banner for my mom because we have missed her so much, and we are very proud of her. Even though we came to the hospital every day to see my mom, my family really missed her being at home.

The doctor talked to my family and said, "Your mom has to be careful not to do too much work around the house because her body is still healing."

I said to Kyle, "We need to help with chores around the house such as laundry, cooking, and cleaning."

Kyle agreed, "Yes Kailey, we have to be very helpful for Mom."